MOG'S
Christmas
Calamity

Judith Kerr

HarperCollins *Children's Books*

First published in paperback in Great Britain
by HarperCollins Children's Books in 2015

1 3 5 7 9 10 8 6 4 2

ISBN: 978-0-00-816436-2

HarperCollins Children's Books is a division of HarperCollins Publishers Ltd.

Text and illustrations copyright © Kerr-Kneale Productions Ltd 2015

Visit our website at www.harpercollins.co.uk

Printed and bound in Italy

MIX
Paper from
responsible sources
FSC® C007454

FSC is a non-profit international organisation established to promote the
responsible management of the world's forests. Products carrying the FSC
label are independently certified to assure consumers that they come
from forests that are managed to meet the social, economic and
ecological needs of present and future generations.

Find out more about HarperCollins and the environment at
www.harpercollins.co.uk/green

One night Debbie said, "Do you know, Mog, when you wake up in the morning it will be Christmas, and there will be presents and lovely things to eat, and you will have an extra big egg for your breakfast."

Mog dreamt about the big egg. It was very big, and it was up in the sky. Mog had to fly up to get it. But some big birds came.

They wanted to eat the big egg, and one
of them wanted to eat Mog. Mog flew as
fast as she could, but the bird came after
her, and suddenly…

She woke up.

Something was stuck to her tail.
She tried to shake it off,
but it stuck on.

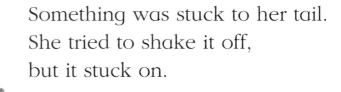

And then it went into the fire,

and made a little fire of its own,

and two more fires on the rug.

Mog thought, "I'm getting out."

She ran out into the street.
Some people saw her shoot past.

"What's that thing
with the fiery tail?"
said one.
"Perhaps it's a comet,"
said another.
"I'd better ring the fire
brigade," said a third.

Suddenly Mog heard a horrible noise.

Then she saw the thing that made the horrible noise.

She thought, "Oh no. I'm going home."

But the thing came after her.
It chased her all the way to her house.

Two men jumped out.
They had a big yellow snake,
and they shouted, "There's
the fire!"

Suddenly the snake spat.
It did a big spit, and there
was water everywhere.

Even on Mog.

Then Mr and Mrs Thomas and Debbie and Nicky came out of the house. They did not come out of the door. They came out of the window.

They said, "Thank you, thank you for saving
our house."
The firemen said, "Don't thank us, thank your cat.
That cat led us to your house. That cat is a hero."

Some neighbours had come to see what had
happened to Mog's house. They all told each other
that Mog was a hero. Then it began to snow and
they all went home.

Mr and Mrs Thomas, Debbie and Nicky
went to get dressed. Then they looked at
the Christmas room.

Everything was wet and some things were black. "I'm sorry," said Mr Thomas, "but Christmas will have to be a bit different this year."

They were all very sad.

Mog was sad too.

But
then
Nicky
saw
something.

The neighbours were coming back.
They were carrying things and smiling.
They said, "We thought we'd help you clean up,
and then we'd all share Christmas at your house."

It was a wonderful party. There were presents
and lovely things to eat and there was even an
extra big egg for Mog.

"That was the best Christmas we ever had," said
Nicky. "Can we do exactly the same next year?"
"Well," said Mr Thomas, "perhaps not exactly."